Stanley at Sea

Written by
Linda Bailey

Illustrated by
Bill Slavin

KIDS CAN PRESS

S tanley knew he wasn't supposed to beg for food. But his people kept eating ... and eating ... and EATING ... and they didn't share a single bite with him. So what else could he do?

He whined. He drooled. He rubbed his cold, wet nose against their legs.

"Stanley!" said his people. "No begging. Get!"

Stanley didn't always understand people talk. But he sure knew "Get!"

He slumped on down to the river. Some of his friends were there — Alice and Nutsy and Gassy Jack. They'd *all* been told to "Get!"

"I'm so hungry, I could eat dirt," said Alice in dog talk.

"I could eat my own tail!" said Nutsy. And for a minute or two, she tried.

Drooling and droopy, the dogs sniffed their way down the path. All they could find was an old wad of gum. It was so dried up, even a *dog* wouldn't eat it.

Then all of a sudden, their noses trembled! Just a few steps away was ...

The most glorious trash can in the world! It was green and gorgeous and packed to the brim with garbage so scrumptious, you wouldn't know where to start.

"There are *burgers* in there!" barked Stanley.

"Tacos!" yipped Nutsy.

"Pizza!" squealed Gassy Jack.

Howling with joy, the dogs ran for the can. But before they could put a single paw on it —

VRROOMM! — out of nowhere came
a huge white truck. Out popped some
claws ... and up went the can!

"Iiiiiiyy!" whined Stanley.

The dogs watched in horror as the
whole magnificent, mouth-watering feast
got *dumped* into the garbage truck.

"Awwrr," moaned the dogs. "Awwrr,
awwrr."

But what could they do?

Not a thing.

Stanley sniffed again.

"Ham!" he barked. "Thataway!"

The dogs raced to a small, red boat. Everyone leaped aboard, but it was Gassy Jack who found the sandwich. In less than a second, he wolfed it down. He ate the lunch bag, too!

The dogs all turned to leave.

But suddenly, everywhere they wanted to walk was ...

Water!

None of the dogs had been on a boat before.

"Are we having a bath?" asked Alice.

"No," said Stanley. "We're not wet."

The only thing they knew was — they were moving!
Houses and bushes and trees raced past. The dogs were
so shocked, they forgot to be hungry.

Up loomed a bridge, crowded with cars. As the dogs drifted closer, the cars all stopped. People jumped out. They pointed and waved.

"Woof!" said Stanley, which in dog talk means "Hi!"

And maybe the people said hi back. But the dogs never knew because, quick as a twitch, they were under the bridge. And right after that, with a whoosh and a whirl ...

The dogs were swept to sea!

"Where are we going?" squeaked Nutsy.

Stanley gazed all around. Outside was *very* big here.
The water was huge, and the sky stretched in every
direction.

"We're going," he cried, "to the end of Outside!"

The other dogs' eyes bugged out. They stared at the water and sky.

"The end of Outside," they said to each other. "Yes!"

"What's there?" asked Alice.

Everyone turned to Stanley. If anyone knew, it was him.

Stanley thought hard. "A fence," he said.

The dogs all barked in agreement. They knew that wherever you go in the world, sooner or later you always come to a fence.

Now that they knew where they were going, the dogs felt better. They bobbed and floated, while all around the air grew thick and white.

Suddenly the air cleared.

"There it is!" yapped Stanley. "The end of Outside!"

The dogs all stared in delight. They had never imagined the fence would be so BIG.

They began to bay with excitement. They leaped and bounced and tumbled — and Nutsy fell into the water!

She let out a frightened yelp. Stanley tried to grab her, but she was too slippery.

Suddenly, from out of the sky, came a man on a rope. He reached out and fished Nutsy from the water. Slowly, he rose, taking Nutsy with him.

Then he came down again. This time he took Alice!

Next was Gassy Jack. And finally, up went Stanley — up, waaaaaaay up, to the top of the fence.

It was *huge* there and full of people. There was room for the dogs to walk and run. But that wasn't the best part.

The best part was that the people on top of the fence had food. Steak and sausages! *And they put it on plates and gave it to the dogs!* When the dogs ate it up, the people brought more steak and sausages. And then even more!

The dogs ate like pigs. They had to waddle away from their plates.

When Stanley finally saw his people again, he was so full of steak and sausage, he could hardly bark.

His people gave him a hug. "Oh Stanley," they said, "where have you *been*?"

"To the end of Outside," thought Stanley. But all he could say was "Erf!"

That's all *any* of the dogs could say. And all they could do on the long ride home was grunt and burp and snore.

But in the days that followed, they talked to their friends, the way dogs do. And they told them the whole story, just as I've told it to you. The story got around ...

And ever since then, dogs have known that if you go to the end of Outside, you will see a very big fence. And if you're lucky, you'll be lifted up, waaaaaaay up to the very top, where you'll be given all the steak and sausages you can eat.

No dog has ever found that fence again ...

... but they *think* about it all the time.

For my mother, Addie Bailey, who has always been curious
about the end of Outside — L.B.

For Nicholas, who came from across the sea — B.S.

Text © 2008 Linda Bailey
Illustrations © 2008 Bill Slavin

Kids Can Press acknowledges the financial support of the Government of Ontario, through the
Ontario Media Development Corporation's Ontario Book Initiative; the Ontario Arts Council; the Canada
Council for the Arts; and the Government of Canada, through the BPIDP, for our publishing activity.

Published in Canada by
Kids Can Press Ltd.
29 Birch Avenue
Toronto, ON M4V 1E2

Published in the U.S. by
Kids Can Press Ltd.
2250 Military Road
Tonawanda, NY 14150

www.kidscanpress.com

The artwork in this book was rendered in acrylics, on gessoed paper.
The text is set in Leawood Medium.

Edited by Debbie Rogosin
Designed by Julia Naimska
Printed and bound in China

This book is smyth sewn casebound.

CM 08 0 9 8 7 6 5 4 3 2

Library and Archives Canada Cataloguing in Publication

Bailey, Linda, 1948–
Stanley at sea / written by Linda Bailey ; illustrated by Bill Slavin.

ISBN 978-1-55453-193-6

1. Dogs—Juvenile fiction. I. Slavin, Bill II. Title.

PS8553.A3644S72 2007   jC813'.54   C2007-902704-0

Kids Can Press is a *Corus*™ Entertainment company